Pickles for Breakfast has been in the idea stage for over 15 years. I'm so excited to finally have it in print!

Thank you, Ryan Lindquist for your valued input and attention to details. In many ways, you were the catalyst to make this book happen. I am grateful.

A special thanks to Sara Fox for agreeing to take this journey with me and for conveying my vision into such fun and lively illustrations!
I hope it leads you to more opportunities.

I also want to thank my husband for his support and encouragement in pursuing my dreams and ideas.

# Pickles for Breakfast

Written by Kim Wendricks

Illustrated by Sara Fox

Sage Frog Press, Wisconsin

Pickles for breakfast,
Pickles for lunch,
Pickles for dinner,
Munch, munch...

CRUNCH!

CRUNCH!

CRUNCH!

They're green and yummy,
Tangy, and crunchy;
They're great for a snack
Or night time munchy.

My first bite of pickle,
I thought, was quite sour!
After several more bites,
I smiled. Pickle power!

Pickles can be sour,
Some can even be sweet.
That first, juicy bite
Truly tickles my feet!

A pickle is a cucumber
That's all dressed up.
Shall we eat them with tea
In a fancy new cup?

Cucumbers grow in gardens
on vines green and strong.
Soon we can make pickles!
I've been waiting so long!

Our secret family recipe,
I shall now create.
Garlic, onion, mustard, and dill;
Oh, boy! I can't wait!

To become tasty pickles,
in brine they must soak.

Are they ready yet?
Let's give them a poke!
PARTY

My friends sell sweet treats
From their sidewalk stands.
I offer large pickles;
They're in high demand!

LEMONADE
BAKE
SALE

Sweet &
SOUR

There are pickles aplenty,
when I'm at the fair;
With so many choices,
would you like to share?

I've seen pickles in a barrel
and pickles in a jar;
Hey!  Wouldn't it be fun
To have a pickle for a car?

My favorite costume
For trick or treat,
Is a giant pickle
With big green feet!

Trips to the market
Make my face smile;
So many options
Are stacked in the aisle!

Some pickles have sugar,
and taste rather sweet;
I will try them on ice cream;
a delightful, new treat!

I do love my pickles,
But eat other things, too;
It's a balancing act
To eat good, healthy food.

LAST SUMMER
3+5=8
MATH
ENGLISH
You could say I love pickles,
that's certainly true;
but to have them for breakfast?
I would! How about you?
TREES
ABCD
HISTORY

# Recipes to make delicious pickles at home!

### Dill Freezer Pickles

8 - cups sliced, slim cucumbers
1 - large sweet onion, sliced
1 - cup vinegar
2 - T. salt
1 - t. celery seed
3 - cloves minced garlic
1 - cup sugar
2 - t. dill weed

Arrange cucumber slices in large crockery mixing bowl (don't use metal or plastic). Measure out enough water to cover them; combine it with salt and add to bowl.

Soak at room temperature 2 hours. Drain, but don't rinse.

Dissolve sugar in vinegar. Pour over cucumbers and lightly mix. Place cucumbers and brine in clean freezer containers. Cover tightly and freeze. (This is how they become crisp.) Thaw in a couple of hours at room temperature or overnight in refrigerator. Refrigerate any leftovers.

Makes about 1 quart.

*Note: The thinner you can slice the cucumbers, the better.

### Bread & Butter (Sweet) Freezer Pickles

7 - cups sliced, slim cucumbers
1 - large sweet onion, sliced
2 - T. salt
2 - cups white sugar
1 - cup vinegar
1 - T. mustard seed
1 - T. celery seed
½ - t. turmeric

Combine cucumbers and onion; sprinkle with salt, let stand 1 hour.

Combine sugar, vinegar, mustard seed and celery seed; pour over cucumber mixture.
Refrigerate 1 day.

Place in containers, leaving 1" head space; freeze.
Yield: 4 pints.
*NOTE: Can be stored in refrigerator 2 weeks. To serve thaw unopened in refrigerator for 6 hours. Crisp and delicious.

Made in the USA
Monee, IL
16 April 2021

65986646R00026

Jobs
KIDS
DISCOVER
IN PARTNERSHIP WITH
Houghton Mifflin Harcourt

# Jobs at School

Workers do different jobs. People do different jobs at your school.

Where do these school workers do their job?

I'm a teacher.

My job is teaching.

I'm a principal.

I'm in charge of the whole school.

I'm a cafeteria worker.

I make and serve the meals.

I'm a librarian.

I help you find a book you may like.